To Elizabeth and Allison—
May your books
be many
and your fines few.

Thanks to Elizabeth, Lee, Hanna,
Lee, Elizabeth, Mike, Laurie,
Susan, Steve, Betsy and
Allison, Ian, Elizabeth,
Jacob, Elizabeth, Peter,
Elizabeth, Lee, Halsey,
and Becky.

SIMON & SCHUSTER BOOKS FOR YOUNG READERS An imprint of Simon & Schuster
Children's Publishing Division 1230 Avenue of the Americas, New York, New York 10020
 SIMON & SCHUSTER BOOKS FOR YOUNG READERS is a trademark of Simon & Schuster. Book design
by Lisa Campbell Ernst. The text for this book is set in Goudy Old Style. The illustrations are rendered in pastel,
ink, and pencil. Printed in Singapore. First Edition. 10 9 8 7 6 5 4 3 2 1
Library of Congress Cataloging-in-Publication Data   Ernst, Lisa Campbell.   Stella Louella's runaway book / by Lisa
Campbell Ernst.   p.   cm.   Summary: As she tries to find the book that she
must return to the library that day, Stella gathers a growing group of
people who have all enjoyed reading the book.
ISBN 0-689-81883-1 [1. Books and reading—
Fiction. 2. Lost and found possessions—Fiction.
3. Librarians—Fiction.] I. Title.
PZ7.E7323St 1998   [E]—dc21   97-33054

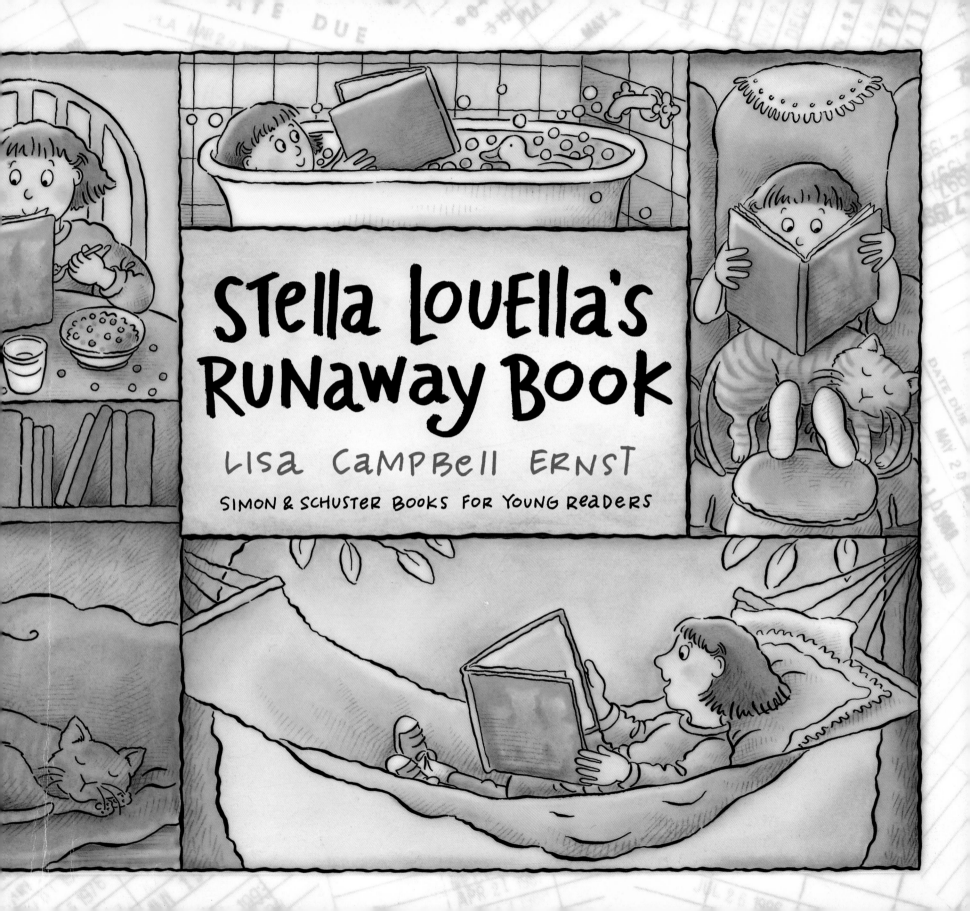

Stella Louella's Runaway Book

Lisa Campbell Ernst

SIMON & SCHUSTER BOOKS FOR YOUNG READERS

On Saturday morning Stella's library book disappeared, as if in a magic act.

Stella was in a tizzy. She ran through the house searching frantically for the book, looking in the backs of closets, on the tops of shelves, in beds, baskets, and bathtubs. She looked in toy boxes, toolboxes, even cereal boxes. The book was gone.

"Great balls of fire!" shouted Stella's father. "What's going on?"

"My library book has disappeared!" Stella cried. "It's due today by five o'clock—how will I *ever* tell Mrs. Graham at the library that I've lost it?" Stella burst into tears.

"Simmer down," her father said. "Think. Where did you have it last?"

Stella squeezed her eyes closed and thought. "The hammock out back!" she gasped.

Stella ran to the hammock with her father close behind. The book was not there. Her little brother, Sam, sat digging in the dirt below.

"Sam!" their dad said. "Stella's library book is missing. It's due today by five o'clock—have you seen it?"

"Yesterday." Sam nodded. "It was a good book. I liked the bears."

"Where is it now?" asked Stella.

"I left it on the front porch," Sam answered, "by the mailbox."

Stella ran to the front porch with Sam and her father close behind. No book in sight. Just then, Wally Hanson walked up.

"Mr. Hanson!" Sam called. "My sister's library book is lost—it has to get back to the library by five o'clock—have you seen it?"

"That was *yours?*" Wally groaned. "It was mixed in with the mail, and I wasn't sure where it came from. Good book, though, especially when they go on a walk."

"Where is it now?" asked Stella anxiously.
"I left it at the house on the corner," he said.
"I thought it might belong to the little girl
who lives there, Tiffany Anne."

Stella ran to the corner house with Wally, Sam, and her father close behind. "Mrs. Graham will be furious with me!" Stella moaned.

Tiffany Anne was sitting on the steps, combing her hair. "Tiffany Anne!" called Wally. "We're looking for Stella's library book—it's due today by five o'clock—did you find it?"

"Hey, great book," said Tiffany Anne. "I *loved* the little girl."

"Where is it?" begged Stella.

"I thought it might have been reported missing," Tiffany Anne said, "so I gave it to Officer Tim when he walked by."

Stella ran all the way to the police station with Tiffany Anne, Wally, Sam, and her father close behind.

"Officer Tim! Officer Tim!" yelled Tiffany Anne. "Do you still have that book I gave you? It's Stella's, and it absolutely *must* get to the library by five o'clock!"

"Uh, negative," said Officer Tim. "I was on my way to return it, but I stopped by Wanda Lynn's Diner to apprehend a cup of coffee, and accidentally left it there. Interesting book, though—a classic case of unlawful entry. Better check the premises to see if it's still there!"

Stella ran fast and furious to Wanda Lynn's Diner with Officer Tim, Tiffany Anne, Wally, Sam, and her father close behind. "Mrs. Graham won't let me check out a book ever again!" Stella fretted.

"Wanda Lynn!" barked Officer Tim. "Have you seen a library book?"

"It was here a minute ago," she said. "*Loved* the part about the porridge."

"But where is it now?" pleaded Stella. "It's due at the library by five o'clock. You know how Mrs. Graham hates late books!"

"Sorry, honey lamb," Wanda Lynn said. "I seem to remember Sal from the fix-it shop picking it up."

Stella ran pell-mell to Sal's Fix-it Shop with Wanda Lynn, Officer Tim, Tiffany Anne, Wally, Sam, and her father close behind.

"Sal, Sal!" shouted Wanda Lynn. "Where is that book you picked up? Stella must get it back to the library by five o'clock!"

"Riveting book," Sal said. "Especially when that chair was broken."

"Please, oh please," begged Stella, "say you still have it here!"

"I'm afraid not," Sal said. "Morty from the Bed Bazaar asked to borrow it."

Stella ran to the Bed Bazaar
with Sal, Wanda Lynn, Officer Tim,
Tiffany Anne, Wally, Sam, and her
father close behind.

"Morty!" called Sal. "We've got a problem.
That book you borrowed is Stella's and it's due at
the library no later than five o'clock today!"

Morty shook his head.
"A baby carried it off not ten
minutes ago! We just might be able
to catch her—she's headed west on Elm
Street with her mother."

"It was a terrific book," Morty raved
as he joined the crowd. "I loved the part
where the little girl tries out the beds!"

Stella moaned. "Mrs. Graham
will *never* believe this!"

Stella ran west on Elm Street with Morty and Sal,
Wanda Lynn, Officer Tim, Tiffany Anne, Wally, Sam, and
her father close behind. It was now three o'clock.

"Stop! Stop!" shouted Morty when they
saw a baby carriage up ahead. "We need that
book back—Stella's got to have it to the
library by five o'clock!"

The mother turned around. "I'm so
sorry, dear," she said to Stella. "It was a
lovely book, especially the part about
the nap. We gave it to a trustworthy
troop of scouts headed south on
Sycamore Street."

"What if I'm banned from the
library?" sobbed Stella. The baby,
too, began to cry.

Stella ran south on Sycamore Street with the baby and mother, Morty and Sal, Wanda Lynn, Officer Tim, Tiffany Anne, Wally, Sam, and her father close behind.

Two blocks later they spied the scouts. "Hey, wait up!" yelled the baby's mother. "There's been a mistake—that library book is Stella's, and it's due by five o'clock today!"

The weary scouts were returning from a long nature walk. "We don't have it," said the exhausted scout leader. "It was a good one, though, especially when the bears finally returned home." The scouts all nodded. "We left it with Duff Morten—he stopped off at the park to work on his bug badge."

"I'll never get to read a library book again!" whined Stella.

Stella ran willy-nilly
toward the park with the troop of
scouts, the baby and mother, Morty and Sal,
Wanda Lynn, Officer Tim, Tiffany Anne, Wally, Sam,
and her father close behind. It was now four o'clock.

"Duff! Quick!" shouted the scout leader. "Hand over that book—it has to get to the library by five o'clock!"

Duff looked up from his magnifying glass. "Ah *ha*," he said. "Excellent book. Especially when the bears discovered that girl. But I gave it to Miss Flynn, the gym teacher, when she ran by. She was headed north!"

Stella now ran north with
Duff Morten, the troop of
scouts, the baby and mother, Morty and
Sal, Wanda Lynn, Officer Tim, Tiffany Anne,
Wally, Sam, and her father close behind.
"Stop!" shouted Duff when Miss Flynn was in sight.
"Stella has to return that library book you have by five o'clock!"

"But I *don't* have
it," said Miss Flynn, still jogging. "I loved
the ending, though, when that little girl
ran through the forest. I left the book on
a bench at the corner of Tenth and Walnut.
Maybe it's still there!"

"I'll probably have to turn in my library
card!" sobbed Stella, still leading
the way.

So Stella ran to the corner of Tenth and Walnut with Miss Flynn, Duff Morten, the troop of scouts, the baby and mother, Morty and Sal, Wanda Lynn, Officer Tim, Tiffany Anne, Wally, Sam, and her father close behind. But when they arrived there, the bench was empty. Everyone searched from top to bottom. Stella's book simply wasn't there.

What they did discover, though,
was that the bench at Tenth and Walnut
was smack dab in the front of the library.
It was ten minutes till five o'clock.

"I guess that's that," Stella said,
choking back the tears. "It's gone. I
might as well go in and confess to
Mrs. Graham. She will never, *ever*
forgive me."

Stella now walked—as slow
as molasses—into the library
with, well, *everyone* close behind.
She thought about turning
around and running, but it was
no use. Mrs. Graham would
track her down eventually.

Then all too soon, Stella was at the front desk. She couldn't bear to look Mrs. Graham in the eye—wonderful Mrs. Graham, who had story hour every Saturday, wonderful Mrs. Graham, who always helped her find books, wonderful Mrs. Graham, whom she was about to disappoint terribly. "I, I've lost my library book," Stella whispered at last, trying not to cry. "I'm so very sorry."

Mrs. Graham smiled mysteriously, pulling something from under the counter. "For some strange reason *this* was on the bench outside," she said.

"My book!" Stella yelled. "You found it!"

Joyful shouts burst from Stella's friends, and there was an excited buzz as everyone recalled their favorite parts again. Mrs. Graham agreed with them all.

"What's *your* favorite part of the book?" Stella asked her.

"Why, the same as with every book," Mrs. Graham said with a chuckle, "my favorite part is when someone READS it!"

So at five minutes till five o'clock, Mrs. Graham checked out a new book to Stella—and Miss Flynn, Duff Morten, the troop of scouts, the baby and mother, Morty and Sal, Wanda Lynn, Officer Tim, Tiffany Anne, Wally, Sam, and her father were all close behind.